**To Mom and Pop
for making everything into a good story—
even this!**

First edition 2009

Library of Congress Cataloging-in-Publication Data is available.

Library of Congress Catalog Card Number 2008938400

ISBN 978-0-7636-3242-7

2 4 6 8 10 9 7 5 3 1

Printed in China

This book was typeset in Symbol.
The illustrations were done in acrylic.

Candlewick Press
99 Dover Street
Somerville, Massachusetts 02144

visit us at www.candlewick.com

The Patterson Puppies

and
the Rainy Day

LESLIE PATRICELLI

CANDLEWICK PRESS

It was a rainy, rainy day,
and the Patterson puppies
had run out of
things to do.

Andy had read his favorite dinosaur book from front to back for the fifty-first time.

Penelope had sorted her hair clips into neat little rows.

Zack had tried on every superhero costume he had. (He'd even put his underwear on his head.)

Petra had told all her stuffed animals their favorite stories and put them to bed.

So they sat.

And sat.

And sat.

And sat.

And sat.

Andy said, "I wish it was sunny."

"Yeah!" said Penelope. "If it was sunny and
warm, I could wear my pretty bathing suit
with the sparkly star on the front!"

"And we could go to the beach," said Zack.
"And if a shark attacked us,
I would get it with my super-strength!"

Then Petra had an idea. . . .

"Let's *pretend* we're at the beach," she said.
"We can have a beach party inside!"

The puppies got to work. They laid out some
beach towels and sand toys and put on some surf music.
Mama brought snacks and teacups filled with water.

Then they all put on their bathing suits.

It was fun! They ate and danced and did the limbo.
Andy danced right into a teacup and tipped it over.

Whoopsie!

Andy looked at the puddle.
He noticed something very interesting.

"Look! A tiny ocean!" he said.

The other puppies looked.
It did look like a tiny ocean!

They all took turns splashing.

It wasn't big enough for all of them, though,
so Penelope thought of a way to make it bigger.

"It's working!" she said.

Then the four little puppies set to work.
Bucket after bucket after bucket of water
splashed onto the blue carpet.

Finally, Penelope declared it finished.
"It's a real ocean!"
she said.

And to the four little puppies,
it really was!

My sister can be crabby
Sometimes, too.

Wheeee!

LAND HO!

Until . . .

The Patterson puppies
had a lot to do the rest
of that rainy day.

They mopped with towels; they mopped with mops.
They mopped and mopped and mopped and mopped.
Papa set up fans to blow the carpet dry.

That night, the puppies were very tired.
Mama made them a bowl of popcorn, and they sat
on the floor to watch their favorite TV show before bed.
With all the fans on, it was cold. So they bundled up.

Everyone was happy, except Andy.
"Petra, you're hogging all the popcorn!" he said.

He pushed her hand away, and
the bowl tipped over.

The fans blew the popcorn into the air.

Andy looked as it swirled around.
He noticed something very interesting.
"It looks like snow!"
he said.

It certainly did.